IF I
COULD BE A
CIRCUS CLOWN

Written and Illustrated by J. Ellen Dolce

MODERN PUBLISHING
A Division of Unisystems, Inc.
New York, New York 10022

If I could
      be a circus clown . . .

I'd walk on my hands
all around town.

And if I could
run the park . . .

I'd let kids play
till after dark.

Well, if I could
    bake a loaf of bread . . .

I'd like to wear it
on my head.

But, if I could
    deliver all the mail . . .

I'd carry it in
a big red pail.

If I could
fix old beat-up cars . . .

I'd sell them
    on the planet Mars.

And if I could
   build big roads . . .

I'd make them safe
    for hopping toads.

Well, if I could
lead a marching band . . .

I'd wear a mitten
        on my hand.

But our job is
just to grow . . .

why does it seem
       so very slow?